Catharine Trotter Cockburn

Olinda's Adventures: The Amours of a Young Lady

e-artnow 2021

Catharine Trotter Cockburn

Olinda's Adventures: The Amours of a Young Lady

e-artnow, 2021
Contact: info@e-artnow.org

ISBN 978-80-273-4198-6

Contents

LETTER I.   12

LETTER II.   16

LETTER III.   19

LETTER IV.   22

LETTER V.   26

LETTER VI.   31

LETTER VII.   35

LETTER VIII.   40

The SECOND VOLUME
OF
Familiar Letters
OF
LOVE, GALLANTRY
And several OCCASIONS,
BY THE
WITS *of the Last and Present Age.*
With the best of *VOITURE*'s Letters, Translated
by Mr. DRYDEN and Mr. T. BROWN.
ALSO THE
REMAINS
Of the Celebrated
Mr. **T. BROWN;**
BEING
LETTERS, POEMS and DIALOGUES
on the TIMES, not Printed in his
WORKS.
LONDON,
Printed for **SAM. BRISCOE.** 1718.

Olinda's Adventures:
OR THE AMOURS
Of a Young LADY.
By *Mrs.* TROTTER.

LETTER I.

Dear Cleander,

I Hope I need not tell you how uneasie this tedious Absence makes me; for I must confess as troublesome as I find it, and as much as I Value you, I can't but wish you may be able to guess at it by what you suffer your self: A strange Effect of the highest degree of Friendship; for if I had less for you, I shou'd not so earnestly desire to hear you are in Pain; but such Contradictions are no Mysteries to you, who understand so well the little Niceties of Friendship. That you may see I study nothing more in this Solitude than to oblige you; I've resolv'd to employ most part of my time in complying with that Request you've often made me, of giving you a particular account of all that has happen'd to me in my Life; tho' I fear I shall lose part of that Esteem which you have hitherto preserved for me, by acquainting you with some Passages of it, which yet I hope have nothing in 'em so ill, that the kindness of a Friend mayn't find out something in the Circumstances of the Story to Excuse: For tho' perhaps I have not always been so nicely cautious as a Woman in strictness ought, I have never gone beyond the bounds of solid Virtue. To put all to the hazard then, I will give you a faithful Account of all my Weaknesses. My Father dying, left me when I was very young, to the Tuition of a Mother, who as you know is qualify'd for such a Charge equal to any of her Sex; and she indeed perform'd her part as well as her small Fortune wou'd permit her, which was scarce sufficient to maintain her, in that Rank her Birth had placed her. However, she gave me all the Education that was necessary; but I believe you'll excuse me if I pass over all that occurr'd till I was Thirteen, for about that time I began to fancy my self a Woman, and the more to perswade me to it, I happen'd to be acquainted with a Gentleman whose Name was *Licydon*, who the first or second time I saw him, seem'd to have so much confidence in me, that he told me a long story of his Love, and ever after shew'd me all the Letters he either Writ to, or received from his Mistress: This you must think did not a little please me. and I thought my self as Wise as the Gravest Politician, when he ask'd my Advice in any of his Affairs, especially when I heard him commended by many for a Man of great Parts. One day that we were by our selves, we fell into a Discourse of Womens making Love; he Argu'd that 'twas very unjust to deprive 'em of the satisfaction of discovering a Passion, which they were as much subject to as Men: I said as much against him as I cou'd, but he had more dexterity to manage his Argument than I; so that I was easily brought to agree with him; but said 'twas well that custom was observ'd, since the complaisance which was paid by their Sex to ours, would sometimes oblige 'em to comply contrary to their Inclination; for I cou'd not imagine how they cou'd civily refuse a Lady's Intreaties. He told me if I wou'd write a Declaration of Love to him, he wou'd shew me how it might be Answer'd with a great deal of Respect, without any Love. I consented to do it, and accordingly did the next day, and he return'd me an Answer which satisfied me: This, tho' it may seem a trivial thing, you will find by the sequel, had like to have produc'd but ill Effects. Some time after this, he brought a Friend of his to Visit us, who was of a good Family; but according to the *English* custom of breeding the younger Sons to Trades; he was a Goldsmith, but a great *Beaux*, and one who seem'd to have a Soul above his calling: He ask'd *Licydon* if he had any pretensions to me, which when he assur'd him he had not, he told him he was very glad he had not a Rival in a Friend; for he was hugely smitten, and shou'd need his Assistance in his design; for he had observ'd such an intimacy between us, as gave him Reason to think he had great influence over me; and he was sure he wou'd not deny him, if he was not my Lover. *Licydon* assur'd him he had only a Friendship for me, and that he wou'd use all his Credit with me to perswade me to receive all His Addresses favourably; which he did as soon as he had an opportunity. He said all of him that he could imagine most engaging, and especially of the Violence of his Passion. I was well enough pleas'd with the Love, tho' not with the Lover; for 'tis natural at that unthinking Age to covet a croud of Admirers, tho' we despise them: But I believe I need not confine that Vanity to Youth, many of our Sex are troubled with it, when one wou'd think they were Old enough to be sensible of the Folly, and inconvenience of being continually Courted, and haunted by Men they have an indifference, or perhaps an aversion for For my part I think there is no greater Torment; but I was of another Opinion then, and therefore Rally'd at the Love, and seem'd not to believe it; which I warrant you gave great Encouragement to my new Lover, when he heard of it; for 'tis a great Sign one wou'd be convinc'd. So I'd best prepare my self for an Attack, which I did not expect long: It was begun by a *Billet Doux*, which came first to my Mother's Hands; and when she gave it me, she ask'd what Answer I wou'd return. I told her I was wholly to be Govern'd by her; but if I was to follow my own inclination I wou'd not answer it at all: My Mother reply'd, she thought it fit I shou'd Answer it; for she believ'd I cou'd have no aversion to him, and she did not think it an ill Match, considering my Circumstances. Then I desir'd her to indite a Letter for me, for I saw well enough I shou'd not please her. She gave me a Copy of one, that without saying any thing that was kind, gave him cause enough to despair; but I cou'd not dissemble my Looks and Actions, in which he observ'd so much Coldness, that tho' several Letters pass'd between us, that wou'd have given hopes to a Man the least apt to presume; he was often half an hour with me alone, without speaking one Word to me. At last he complain'd to *Licydon* of the strange contradictions in what I did, and what I Writ; for whenever he begun to speak to me of his Love, I check'd him with such severe Looks, and turn'd the Discourse in such a manner, that he durst proceed no further, tho' my Letters seem'd much to his Advantage. *Licydon* perswaded him (as perhaps he thought himself) that 'twas only my Modesty, and that perhaps I shou'd be more emboldned, if he cou'd get my Mother's consent to his Proposals. *Berontus*, for that was his Name, was as well satisfy'd with this, as if I had told him so my self; and away goes he immediately to my Mother, and tells her he's stark staring mad in Love with her Daughter: The next thing they talk of is Joynture, and Settlements, *&c.* and in fine they agree; So I am call'd for, and commanded to look upon this Spark as one that must shortly be my Husband; to give us the more freedom, my Mother leaves us together. 'Well, Madam, (says he) I have no Opposites to struggle with, your Mother has given me her consent, and you have given me hopes that you will not refuse me yours. What shou'd I do in this perplexity? I had a firm Resolution never to Marry him; but I found my Mother so much set upon it, that I durst not let it be known; besides, I had engag'd my self so far in Obedience to her, that I did not know how to come off; but for the present I wou'd be whimsical, and take time to consider what I shou'd do hereafter. So I put on a pet, and said, *Berontus*, I don't know what advantage you think you have more than before; but I'm sure a Lover wou'd have found another way of Courting his Mistress, than by her Mother; and it may be you'll find your self never the nearer my Heart for having gain'd her: I hate a Man that will depend upon any other for my Favour than my self. 'Cruel Creature, *says he*, what pleasure do you take in tormenting me? You know that I love you with the greatest respect imaginable, and that I can't be happy but by you alone. I never had Recourse to your Mother till you had encourag'd me, and gave me leave to say it; your usage of me is very unjust. I knew well enough he was in the Right; but I wou'd not know it: So that we parted both much dissatisfied. How his Thoughts were employ'd I can't pretend to tell you; but I was continually contriving how to get out of this troublesome Affair. I cou'd find no way but to tell him sincerely, that all that I had writ in his favour was by constraint; that I was too young to think of Love, or Marriage, and so trust to his Generosity; and prevail with him, if possible, to let it fall of his side. The first time I had an opportunity of putting my design in Execution, I thought the poor Lover wou'd never have liv'd to see me beyond those Years which serv'd for a pretence for my refusal; but he was Wise enough to baulk me, 'If, *says he (after he was come out of his Dumps; for he was a quarter of an hour* without saying any thing. You see he was much given to silence) 'If I did not imagine it your Hate that only study'd an Excuse, I shou'd wait with a great deal of satisfaction, till you were pleas'd to make me happy: But as it is, I shall die a thousand times with fear, that some other more happy in your inclinations than I, will rob me of you for ever. He said in fine, abundance of fine things, to perswade me to engage my self to him; but I wou'd not consent to it; and all I could say to him, was as little prevalent to make him desist his suit. He wou'd wait the Patriarch's Prenticeship rather than lose his Angel: Would it not be a sad Business if he should lose her after all? But I am afraid he's like, for her thoughts cannot be brought so low; they towre a little above his Shop, perhaps too high for her Fortune; but she's something too young to consider that, or to prefer her Interest to her Humour. But to go on with my Story; my Mother was well enough satisfied to have the Match delay'd; so that I thought I had nothing to do for a Year or two, but to wish some Accident might intervene to hinder it. But it was not long before a Servant we had in the House found me other Employment; I had complain'd of some Negligences she had been guilty of, when my Mother was out of Town, which were occasion'd by a fondness she had for one that waited upon *Licydon*: Upon which she had been like to be turn'd away, and being of a revengeful Spirit, she cou'd never forgive it. She had observ'd, that *Licydon* often gave me, and I him, Letters in private; for when he had no other opportunity, he us'd to give me those he sent, or receiv'd from his Mistress, as we were taking leave, when I conducted him to the Door; which I often did, whilst my Mother was entertaining other Company; and I return'd 'em when I saw him again. This malicious Wench hoping to find something in 'em that might prejudice me, to *Licydon*'s Man (over whom it seems she had a great Influence) that she heard his Master was a great Poet, and that she had a great mind to see some of his Works, if he could contrive to let her into his Closet when he was abroad: The Servant who suspected nothing, promis'd her he wou'd let her know the first time his Master left his Key, which he very seldom did. He kept his Word with her, and after she had look'd over all his Papers, at last she found that Letter which I spoke of at the beginning. She knew my Hand well enough, and no doubt with Joy, put it into her Pocket, without being perceiv'd by the Fellow; and to lose no time, went presently to *Berontus*; to whom she said, That she was extreamly concern'd to see him deceiv'd by two that he rely'd so much upon, as her young Mistress and *Licydon*: And therefore she could not forbear telling him, that she had discover'd an Intrigue between 'em, and that they were so familiar, that if they were not Married already, she was sure they wou'd be very suddenly; with abundance of Circumstances of her own Invention, to make the Story more plausible. He did not believe her at first; but when she show'd him the Letter, it put him beyond doubt; so that after he had given her his Word, whatever Measures he took, not to discover her, she went away very well pleas'd, that she had depriv'd me of a Husband, and receiv'd a good Reward for it. *Berontus* did not give his Rage and Grief leave to abate; but in the height of both, writ a Letter to *Licydon*, and another to me. You can't imagine how much I was surprized when I read it, and found it was a Chalenge, (for in that Confusion he had mistaken the Direction) to one whom he accus'd of betraying him in what was dearer to him than his Life: I cou'd not guess who it was design'd for, till *Licydon* came in, and show'd me a Letter he had just receiv'd, which he believ'd was for me; and desir'd me to tell him who that happy Man was *Berontus* complain'd so much of. I saw plainly then he was jealous of *Licydon*; but was not able to Divine the Cause: He gave me the Letter which contain'd these Words;

Wou'd to Heaven you had told me Truth, when you said you were too young to think of Love; you have thought of it too much *Olinda,* for my quiet; but you were born to Torment me. It is my Fate, why do I complain of you? Pity me, if I fall by my happy Rivals Hand, and if you can, forgive me if I survive him. This is the last time I design to trouble you: I wish he may be more faithful to you than he has been to me: Adieu, Madam, pity the unfortunate *Berontus.*

The Letter seem'd so full of Distraction, that I cou'd not chuse but pity him; for I really thought him Mad: But I did not think fit to shew *Licydon* that which was design'd for him. When he was gone I sent for *Berontus*, but he refus'd to come, and 'twas with much ado after three or four times sending he was prevail'd with. I told him by what means I had seen both his Letters; but that they appear'd so great Mysteries to me, that I sent for him to explain 'em. 'Twas long before he wou'd let me know the Cause of his suspicions; but I was so importunate, that at last he show'd me the Love Letter I had writ to *Licydon*: Can I have a greater Proof than this, says he? I confess, reply'd I, you have Reason to think as you do; but you are much deceiv'd; and then I told him upon what occasion it was writ: I saw very well he did not believe me, and I knew not how to convince him, unless I cou'd find *Licydon*s Answer, which at least wou'd clear him. I found it by good Fortune, and brought it to *Berontus*. Read this, said I, and you'll see whether it be true, that I Writ to *Licydon* in earnest: You have nothing to accuse him of. After he had read it, he cry'd out in a violent manner, I have wrong'd the innocent *Olinda*, and I deserve to be hated by her for ever. Be not so transported I return'd coldly enough, I may love *Licydon*, tho' he be so indifferent: The Postscript fully clears you, reply'd *Berontus*, and makes me not dare to ask you to forgive me: Upon which I took it, and read these Words, which I had quite forgot. *I did not think one* cou'd write so prettily of Love, and be so insensible of it; How happy wou'd that Man be, that shou'd receive such a one dictated by your Heart, as well as Hand. *I am sure none cou'd return such an Answer to Olinda.* This Complement did me so much Kindness, that one wou'd think I shou'd be a better Friend to 'em than you know I am. *Berontus* left me almost as angry at himself, as he was before at us; and did not come near me for some time after. When I told *Licydon* what had pass'd between us, he was amaz'd: He Examin'd his Man, who had been in the Chamber, who confess'd the Truth; and our Servant, when she was tax'd with it, hardly deny'd it; and thus the whole Matter was discover'd; which had it not been for a happy Mistake, had probably cost one, or both of them, their Lives, and me my Honour. Two days after *Licydon* was Married, and so our Acquaintance broke off; for tho' his Wife came to see me and often press'd me to keep a Correspondence with her; I never did, for I knew she had been very Jealous of me before she Marry'd, and I would not hazard the reviving it. *Berontus* easily obtain'd his Pardon of me (for you know I'm very good Natur'd) and so he continu'd to Visit me, taking all the pains he could to please me, without any thing remarkable happening, till three Monthes after, his Elder Brother, who had been at his Travels, and was reported to be dead, return'd; so that he was no longer able to keep the Conditions he had made with my Mother; for he had nothing to live upon but his Trade; which I afterwards heard he neglected very much, and took to that usual remedy of Cares, Drinking: He said it was to cure his Grief for the loss of his Mistress, and truly that is to be lamented, when the loss of a good Estate is the Cause of it. However he is comforted for both now, and Married to a Woman with a great Fortune. I was very glad to be rid of my Lover, tho' I was sorry 'twas by his misfortune.

Thus *Cleander*, you have an account of the first Adventures of my Life; which made me early know some uneasie Hours: By the next Post I'll acquaint you with a Catalogue of Lovers (that is, they were my *En* passant, *in taking their Rounds, and serv'd better to divert me than* the most Romantick Constancy, without giving themselves, or me any trouble) but it's indeed time to make an end. Adieu my Friend, think of me always, and, Write as often as you can to *Olinda*.

LETTER II.

To proceed in Order to my Relation, I must begin with one, who in respect of his Years as well as the time in which I knew him, demands the Pre-eminence. He was a *Dutch* Coll. about Threescore; Don't you think one of his Country and Years, will make a pretty Lover? But Old as he was, he had a Mistress in the House with him. I was younger than she, and I believe I may say, without Vanity, I had some other Advantages over her; so that the Old Spark had a Month's mind to me; and I, partly to plague her, and partly to divert my self, received all his Addresses with a great deal of complaisance. I cou'd perceive her fret within her self, tho she durst not shew it. She was in great fear of losing him; for the Man's Money had such Charms as aton'd for his want of 'em, tho' he was Ugliness in perfection; (if that ben't Nonsense) and 'twas the best Jest in the World to me, to see him squint an Amorous Glance upon me with one Eye, whilst 'tother was watching whether she took Notice of him; for we Lodg'd in one House together; so that I cou'd not avoid often being with them both, nor indeed did I endeavour it; for I took a malicious pleasure in laughing at their Follies: Since there's nothing so ridiculous as an Antiquated Lover, who has the Vanity to believe he is belov'd, and a Jealous Woman, who has not Discretion enough to hide it. That I might be sufficiently entertain'd with both, one day I began a Discourse of Young and old Lovers, preferring the last as more Constant, more Fond, and more Solid than the First: He Smil'd, and took me by the Hand, and gave me a thousand Commendations for the Wisdom of my choice; Nay, and so far forgot himself, that he apply'd it to himself, and said such passionate things as wou'd have been extravagant from a young Fellow. She with a great deal of Heat contradicted all I had said, and told all the Impertinences and Inconveniences one finds in an Old Man (which she experimentally knew better than I) without considering how far it touch'd him, she was so earnest against me. This made him so Angry, and her so out of Countenance when she reflected so upon what she had said, that I was never better diverted: So she did not know what Excuse to make for her self; and in fine, the Dispute grew so high, that at last they parted. Upon this the Coll. was hotter upon me than ever; he pester'd me continually with his Visits, and the Brute so little understood my Raillery, that he pretended an Interest in me, and wou'd check me when he saw any body younger than himself with me; but I gave him such Answers, that he did not know what to make of me. When he had Orders for *Flanders*, he told me I must prepare my self to go with him, and I should live as great and happy as a Queen; I said I wou'd go withal my Heart, upon Condition his Son should be always with us: The Old Man started, my Son, Child, what would you do with him? I think he is fitter company for me than you, says I, and so I left him, so asham'd, that he shunn'd seeing me ever after. He e'en went to *Flanders* without me, and vow'd, young as he was, he wou'd never have any thing to do with Woman more. Thus I was rid of my Old Impertinent, whose place was soon supply'd by one of those gay youths who never wait for the slow gifts of pity, but Ravish little Favours from us, as if they were their due; who make it impossible for us to think it a Crime to give what they ask with so much boldness; and who are always endeavouring to divert her they design to please. He Courted me with Balls, Musick, and Entertainments, and in the midst of 'em wou'd now and then whisper some pretty Love Maggots. I was first acquainted with him at a Relations of mine at *Greenwich*: He was an Officer in the Army, and was then in the Camp upon *Black-Heath*; and being very well known in the House where I was, he came often there. He had heard several things of me to my Advantage, (for Fame generally flatters or detracts) as, that I sung well, was Handsom, and so forth: And I was told, that he was very well accomplish'd, and the Neatest, Prettiest, Gentilest young fellow that was to be seen in the whole Army: So that we had both a great desire to see one another, and were very well acquainted the first time we met: He told me he had a violent Passion for me, and he did not doubt but I had a little Love for him; he came to see me every Day whilst I was there; carried me to all the Diversions that were to be had about the Country; and when I was going to *London*, he told me he would soon follow me: But as soon as you come to Town, Faith *Olinda*, you shall Write to me, as you hope to see me again; for I can't live without hearing you Arriv'd safe. So I Writ a thousand little mad things, and he Answer'd me at the same Rate, only a great deal of Airy Love mingled with it. The following Week he came to see me, and from that day I was never suffered to rest for one frolick or other: All the time he staid, I liv'd a pleasant sort of a Life, till he went to Fight abroad, and got two or three new Mistresses to divert, for those sort of Men never remember the Absent; their Love never enters the Heart, nor do they often gain ours; they seldom fail to please indeed, and they force us to think of 'em sometimes whether we will or not; but they are neither Discreet, nor Constant enough to go any further: I suppose he forgot me as soon as he left me, and I was not much behindhand with him. After he was gone, I had scarce a breathing time before another of his Profession, more serious, and more designing, succeeded him: He had a good Estate, and pass'd in the World for a Man of Honour, and therefore was Received by my Mother favourably enough. I neither lik'd, nor dislick'd him; but treated him with Civility, till I found out that his designs were not very Honourable; and then I thought it time to alter my Behaviour: I forbid him to see me, and when he came to our Lodgings, I was deny'd to him, tho' he knew I was at home; upon which he left off coming, and when some of his Comrades ask'd him the Reason, he told them, he knew me too well, and that he did not think a Creature so young cou'd be so Lew'd. Observe, my Friend, how unhappy Women are, who are thus expos'd to lose either their Virtue, or their Honour; if I had comply'd with him, perhaps none wou'd have been more careful of my Fame than he: But how much my Choice is to be preferr'd, none but those who have experienced the unexpressible satisfaction it gives can know. I heard of it with a great deal of indifference, and did not so much as hate the Author of the scandal. The next in waiting was a *French* Beaux: *He had a great stock of Wit, but more Vanity, a mighty* Flatterer, and one who took much pains to perswade credulous Women that he lov'd them; and if he succeeded, he always forsook 'em, and sometimes gratify'd his Vanity to their Cost, who had been indiscreet enough to give him occasion. He laid his Baits to catch me, he Vow'd, and Swore, and Danc'd, and Sung eternally by turns; but I was too wary to be caught, tho' he made me a hundred Protestations, I was the only Woman he ever did, or ever cou'd Love; follow'd me where ever I went, and in spite of the greatest Rigour I cou'd use, wou'd not forbear haunting me. I did not know how to free my self from the Impertinence of this Fop; but I thought if I cou'd convince him of one Act of Inconstancy, he wou'd not have the Confidence to trouble me any more: I had many contrivances in Order to it, but at last I fix'd upon one that was probable enough to take with one of his Humour. I Writ a Letter (disguising my Hand) as from a Woman extreamly in Love with him, and desir'd him to tell me sincerely whither he was engaged or not; for I was too just to rob any Woman of his Heart, and too nice to be content with a part of it. I told him if he was free, I wou'd meet him, the next day at the Bird-Cage in the Park: He sent a very obliging answer to the unknown Lady; and said, he was passionately in Love with her Wit; that if her Beauty were Answerable, he must be undone; however 'twould be such a pleasing Ruin, that he waited with the highest impatience for the appointed hour, when he might assure her by word of Mouth, his Heart was wholly at her dispose. Just as I had done Reading this Letter he came in, and for a Proof of his Constancy, shew'd me that which I had sent him, with another, which he said was the Answer he design'd to send; wherein he told her, he was already so deeply in Love, 'twas impossible for him to change; with abundance of fine things of the Person he Lov'd. This was good sport for me, and I had much ado to keep my Countenance; I us'd all my Rhetorick to perswade him to stay with me; a thing I had never desir'd of him before, and now 'twas in vain: He pretended earnest business, and went long before the Hour, he was so very impatient. When he was gone, I chang'd my Clothes, took a Lady with me, who was Privy to the Affair, and went to the aforesaid Place. We were in Masks, and it being duskish, he did not know us; but after I had banter'd him for some time, I discover'd my self: I cannot describe to you the different Passions that affected him; sometimes he was in a Rage with me for putting such a Deceit upon him, sometimes he wou'd frame weak Excuses for what he had done, and sometimes he was not able to speak at all for Grief, that he was not only disappointed of a new Mistress, but had lost all hopes of gaining one he had

Courted so long, with so much Assiduity. I went home, as well pleas'd with losing one, as I have sometimes been with making a Conquest, in full hopes I shou'd be plagued with him no more, and I was not deceiv'd. You see, *Cleander*, what a Miscellany of Lovers, if I may call 'em so, I have had, all of different humours, but none that had found out the Secret to please me: They have done enough if they contribute any thing to your diversion, and made a sufficient Recompence for all their former Impertinence to

Your faithful Friend

Olinda.

LETTER III.

My Friend,

THE Reflections you made upon my two last are so Just, so Profitable, and so Pleasant, that thro' them I see the Author's great Capacity, that can make so good use of such little things; and while I read, bless my kind Fate that made you my Friend, when the Good and Wise are so scarce; and wonder how so particular a Blessing came to be my Lot; which more than doubly satisfies for all I suffer'd by *Clarinda's* falseness. I believe you think it strange I never mention'd her, in any of the Passages of my Life, since it was before many that I have told you of, that I knew and lov'd her: But I could not have Nam'd her without some Marks of kindness, that I either show'd, or receiv'd from her, which I would willingly forget, and cou'd not now speak of her, but when I put your Friendship in compensation with her Ingratitude. But since I am fall'n upon this Subject, I will let you know a little better than you do, the only Woman that I ever trusted, not with any Secret, for you see I then had none of consequence; but with my Love, and in that she betray'd me. Her Sister often told me, she was sorry to see so sincere a Friendship bestow'd upon one that knew so little how to Value it; that *Clarinda* was the same to all, which she pretended to be only for me: That she was always fondest of her new acquaintance, and wou'd Sacrifice, or Ridicule the Old, the better to Caress 'em: But I knew there had been some Quarrels betwixt them, and therefore wou'd not believe it, till I found it too true; and then my partiality for her, chang'd into as great an Error on the other hand, for I involv'd the whole Sex in her Faults, and with *Aristotle* (I hope one may condemn one's self with *Aristotle*) Repented that I had ever Trusted a Woman. I don't know whether I forgot I was one, or whither I had the Vanity to think my self more perfect than the rest; but I resolv'd none of the Sex was capable of Friendship; and continu'd in that Opinion till I knew *Ambrisia*, who (if one may judge by the Rule of Contraries, convinces me of injustice) for she is just *Clarindas* Antipodes. *Clarinda* loves new Faces, and professes a particular kindness at first sight; *Ambrisia* is a long time before she goes beyond Civility, and never does but to those whom she has well observ'd, and found 'em Worthy: *Clarinda* will Rail at one Friend to engage another: *Ambrisia* can't hear an innocent person, tho' her Enemy, accus'd without defending 'em: *Clarinda* will be one day fond to extravagance, and the next as indifferent for the same person: *Ambrisia* is always the same, and where once she loves, she never changes: *Clarinda* is easily angry: *Ambrisia* is perhaps too mild. *Clarinda* has Wit indeed, but 'tis not temper'd by Judgment, so that it makes her often do, and say a hundred things that call her discretion in question: *Ambrisia* has a Solid and piercing Judgment, one wou'd think all she says was the Result of premeditation, she speaks such Wise and such surprizing things, and yet her Answers are so ready, that one wou'd Swear she did not think at all; her Actions are always most regular; I believe she never cou'd accuse her self of an imprudent one. This is a true and unprejudic'd Character of both; and if you wonder how I cou'd love a Woman with such gross Faults, I must tell you, some of them I did not know then; some I excus'd, for I did not expect perfection, and some my partial kindness made me cover with the Name of some Neighbouring Virtue. You know, *Ambrisia* has as great advantages of *Clarinda* in Body as in Mind: I have often heard you praise her outward Beauty, and now I have shew'd you the Beauties of her Soul, tho' they are far greater than I can express, give me leave to wish her yours. Forgive me if I mingle a little self-Interest in my wishes for you, I can't resist a thought of joy for the hopes of finding two Noble Friends in one, by such a happy Union: Think of it *Cleander*; you only deserve one another. I know you will bid me take your advice, and shew you the way; but I shall tell you things that will convince you, my refusal is reasonable. I was just fifteen years old when a particular Friend of my Mothers buried her Husband; whose Grief was so great, that my Mother durst hardly leave her; she staid with her Night and Day, and manag'd all her Affairs for her. She went to *Cloridon's*, who had had a Friendship for the Deceas'd; (for they were forc'd to make use of that, and his Authority in a business, wherein the Widdow had lik'd to be wrong'd) but Men of his Quality are not always at Leisure, and must be waited on; so that tho' my Mother went two or three times, she did not see him, and having other Affairs of her own, and her Friends in hand, besides being oblig'd to be much with her, she cou'd not Watch his Hours: However 'twas a thing of too great consequence to be neglected: So she Writ a Letter to him, and Order'd me to carry it, and to deliver it into his own Hand. I went often to his Lodgings before I cou'd speak with him, and carry'd *Clarinda* with me: At last I was appointed an hour when I shou'd certainly meet with him, and she happen'd to be so engag'd, she cou'd not possibly go with me. I knew no body else I cou'd use so much freedom with, and was forc'd to go alone. I did not wait long before I was admitted, and he approach'd me with that awful Majesty which is peculiar to him; and that commands respect from all that see him. Whilst he held the Letter I gave him, I look'd at him sometimes; but still I met his Eyes, so that I cou'd not view him well, tho' I saw enough to think him the Charming'st Man in the World: He ask'd my Name, and whose Daughter I was? which when I told him, he said he knew my Father very well; that he was a Worthy Man, and that for his sake he wou'd do any thing for me that lay within his Power. I thank'd him, tho' I took it for a Courtier's Complement, and desir'd an Answer to the business I came about. *I will go my self instantly*, says he, *to see what can be* done in it, and give you an Account of it in the Afternoon; but there's so much Company at my Lodgings, that 'tis not a convenient place for you: Can't you come somewhere else? *Yes my Lord,* says I, *very* innocently, where you please: *if you will be in a Hackney Coach then,* at Five a Clock by *Covent-Garden* Church, I will come to you, and let you know what I can do for your Friend. *I told him I would, and went* away very well satisfy'd with him, for I had no apprehensions of any design, from a Man of his Character. You know all the World thinks him the fondest Husband upon Earth, and that he never had a thought of any Woman but his Wife, since he Marry'd her. This made me secure, and I did not fail to go at the appointed hour. My Mother knew nothing of it till afterwards; for I did not see her that day. When he came to me, he told me, what he had done; inform'd himself of some things that were necessary for him to know, that related to the business, and assur'd me he wou'd do the Widow Justice. Then he renew'd his Promise to me with Protestations, that I shou'd command him as far as his Authority or Interest cou'd go; and beg'd me to make use of him either for my Relations, or my self, when ever I had occasion. After he had made me some Speeches of my Wit and Beauty, we parted, and as soon as I saw my Mother, I told her all that pass'd between us. She was extreamly pleas'd to have so great a Man her Friend; especially, one that she had no Reason to suspect of any ill Design, since he had taken no advantage of so favourable an opportunity as I had given him to discover himself, if he had any; nor had not so much as desir'd to continue the Correspondence. The next day the business was concluded more to our satisfaction than was expected. Sometime after this, a Gentleman of my Mothers acquaintance told her, he had a mind for a Commission in the Army, and that he would give a considerable sum of Money to any Body that would procure it. My Mother said she'd try her Interest, and made me Write to *Cloridon* about it. He sent me an obliging Answer, and desir'd to see me at the same Place where we met before, that I might give him an exact Account of the Person I recommended, and Answer some Questions about him more particularly than I cou'd do by Writing. I did so in the first part of our Conversation; and then he began to talk of the many ills that Attend greatness, of which he said Flattery was the chief; for it was the greatest Unhappiness to be sooth'd in ones Faults: *But* Olinda, continu'd he, *in you I see all that Sincerity and* Ingenuity that is requisite for a Friend, and I shou'd think my self very Happy, if you wou'd let me see you sometimes; if you wou'd tell me of my Faults, and what the World says of me. *You Honour me too much my* Lord, *says I,* but you have taken such care to make all Virtues your own, that there's no room left for Flattery, or Correction. To be short, after a great many Compliments of this Nature he told me, 'twou'd be an Act of so great goodness, that he was sure I cou'd not deny him. But what will the World think, *says I,* of such private Meetings? *If* neither you, nor I, tell it, it won't be known, *says he,* as it should if I came to Visit: you. So that I may have the same Innocent Pleasure of seeing you, which you wou'd not deny me in Publick, without making any Noise: And since I assure you I have only a Friendship for you, it can't shock your

Virtue. *I neither granted, nor deny'd him his Request;* for I did not know whither I shou'd do the first, and cou'd not resolve to do the last; both because it might be a hindrance to our business, and because I was very well pleas'd with his Conversation. Nothing cou'd be more agreeable; he is a Man of as much Sense, and as great Address, as any I ever knew: But what is more to be commended and wondred at in a Statesman, he never promis'd any thing that he did not perform. He gave me his Word for the Commission I desir'd; appointed me a day when I shou'd meet him to receive it; and kept it punctually. These were such great Obligations, that I cou'd not but have some acknowledgments for 'em. There was nothing talk'd of in our House, but *Cloridon's* Generosity; and about that time, all the Town rung of some great Actions he had then perform'd: So that all things Contributed to encrease my Esteem of him. I Writ him a Letter of Thanks, and he told me in his Answer, that he desir'd no other Recompence for all he cou'd do for me, but to see me sometimes. I consider'd, that there was no danger in seeing a Man, that was so great a Lover of his Lady; and that profess'd only a Friendship for me: That if ever he shou'd change, I cou'd easily forbear it, and that whatever happen'd, my Virtue was a sufficient Guard. So I consented to it, without letting my Mother know any thing of it. But I must delay telling you what these secret Meetings produc'd; for time and Paper fails me, and will scarce give me leave to assure you that I am

Your tenderest Friend

Olinda.

LETTER IV.

You wou'd pity rather than chide me, *Cleander*, if you knew the Cause of my not Writing to you all this while. I have not been one moment alone for this Fortnight past, but condemn'd to entertain a mix'd company, all of different Humours, different ways of Living, and of Conversing; so that 'twas almost impossible to please one without Contradicting anothers Humour. You may judge how uneasie this was to me; for I've often told you, I had rather be all my Life alone, than with a Company that is not chosen: That I sometimes prefer Solitude even to the best, and that I had now retir'd to avoid the World: But I find one never enjoys any thing without disturbance that one places one's happiness in; and I was to blame to expect a singular Fate shou'd be cut out for me. But whatever Accident deprives me of any thing else I Love, I can never be unfortunate, if *Cleander* continues to be my Friend. You may remember I broke off my last, where I had resolv'd to see *Cloridon*, as he desir'd. We met as often as we cou'd, extreamly to both our satisfactions: He told me all his little uneasinesses, and had so great a Confidence, in me, that he discover'd some Intreagues of State to me, that are yet unknown to some that think they are not strangers to the most secret transactions of the Court; and he never undertook any of his own Affairs of greatest moment, without asking my Advice. Thus we liv'd for two Months, and nothing past that gave me Reason to repent an Action, that was not ill in it self; but might be so by the Consequences of it, till one day, when he had been telling me several things which concern'd him nearly: *But there's one Secret*, says he, Olinda, *that I have never told you yet, tho' it takes up all* my Heart: But 'tis that I believe you know it too well already. *I said,* I cou'd not so much as guess at it. *What*, Olinda *interrupted, is it* possible you shou'd be Ignorant, that I am the most in Love of any Man in the World? How cou'd you imagine, I that knew you so well cou'd have only a Cold Respect or Friendship for you? No no, *Olinda,* I Love you; I love you Ardently; I cannot live unless you give me leave to tell you so; and to hope that you will one day return it. *I was so amaz'd at* this Discourse, I did not know what to Answer: It vex'd me to be oblig'd to alter my way of Living with him; but I did not find my self so Angry at his Love as I ought. However, I disguis'd my thoughts, and put on all the Severity that is needful in such Cases. I have more Reason to be displeas'd with such a Declaration from you my Lord, *said I*, than any other: You that say you knew me so well; What have you seen in me to Encourage it? Have I ever given you occasion to suspect my Virtue? Or is it that you are tired with my Conversation, and therefore take this most effectual means to be freed from it? *Inhumane Fair!* said he, *Must you* hate me because I love you? can you Resolve not to let me see you, only because you know I desir'd it more than before? *In short, he said the* most passionate things that a Lover can imagine; and tho' I found he mov'd my Heart too much, I dissembled well enough to hide it from him. Nothing he said, cou'd prevail with me to see him, and I hop'd Absence wou'd help me to forget him. He Writ many melancholly Letters to me, telling me all the Court took notice of his Grief; that it would shortly be his death, if I would not see him; and beg'd me to live with him as I had done, and he wou'd never speak to me of his Love. But still I refus'd, tho' unwillingly. I was Angry at my self for thinking of him, and for being pleas'd, when some told in Company where I was, that he had been so out of Humour for some time, that no Body durst speak to him of Business. I lov'd to think it was for me, and ask'd a hundred Questions about him. But now the Publick Affairs oblig'd him to go to *Flanders*, where he perform'd Actions Worthy of himself. His Valour, Generosity, and Liberality were talk'd of everywhere, which still more and more engag'd me. I cou'd not but have some Inclination for so fine a Man, when I consider'd that he lov'd me too: However, I believ'd I had only that Esteem for him which I thought due to his Merit, and that Gratitude which the Obligations I had to him requir'd. But I grew insensibly more Melancholy than Usual. One Evening that my Mother and I were taking a serious Walk by the Canal in St. *James's* Park, a Gentleman of her Country, and Acquaintance, seeing us at a distance, came to bear us Company: The Air being pretty Cool, we wore our Masks, and after we had made two or three Turns, he saw a Friend of his, of the same Nation, coming towards us. *That*, says he, *is* Antonio, *Son to* my Lord —- He is a very well Accomplish'd Gentleman, and has a good Estate, I wish he were Married to *Olinda. I know the Family, and have* hear'd of him, *Replyed my Mother*, I shou'd not dislike the Match. By this time he was come up to us, and after having beg'd Pardon for intruding, and leave to Walk with us, he turn'd of my side. He had not seen my Face, for it was duskish, and I only made a Fashion of lifting my Mask upon our first Compliments; but yet he said abundance of fine things, of my Beauty and Charms. After half an Hours Conversation we were going home, and they would needs wait upon us, but one of his Servants met him, and told him he had been looking for him a long time; some Friends of his that were going out of *England* the next day, staid for him in the Mall, and must speak with him immediately. So he left us to the others Care, and went back. The first time *Antonio* met with his Friend, with whom he had seen us; he told him, he was so Charm'd with the Ladies Conversation, that he could not rest till he saw her again. He Answer'd, that he wou'd not like her if he had seen her, but he wou'd carry him to Visit one, whose Beauty wou'd soon make him forget her. *Antonio* said that Wit and good Humour had far greater Charms for him, than the finest Face in the World: But that you mayn't think me obstinate, I will see her upon condition, that if her Eyes have not that influence which you expect, you will make me acquainted with that Lady whose Wit has engag'd me more perhaps than you imagine. He promis'd he wou'd, and so left him, and came to our Lodging: He gave us an Account of this Conversation, and desir'd us to continue the Humour, and not let him know we had seen him before; for he fancy'd a great deal of Pleasure in seeing me Rival my self. We agreed to it, and when they came, I entertain'd him with the greatest simplicity imaginable: For you must know I had an Aversion for him, which I cou'd give no Reason for (that Passion is as unaccountable as Love) and therefore I was pleas'd he shou'd think me a Fool, that he might not desire to see me again. I was glad to perceive he was uneasie in my Company, and to make him the more so, I talk'd very much, and very little to the purpose. When he was gone, he said to his Friend, *That if* Olinda *had the other Ladies* Soul, she wou'd be a dangerous Person; but that as she was, he cou'd no more Love her than a fair Picture: That her Folly had only made him the more eager to see the unknown, and therefore he claim'd his Promise. *He Answer'd*, that he did not know what a second sight of *Olinda* might do; but however not to be worse than his Word, he wou'd endeavour to contrive a Meeting, but he cou'd not promise he shou'd see her Face, for she was very shy of that, as she had some Reason. I was extreamly averse to seeing him again, but this Gentleman was so earnest with me, and my Mother said so much for it, for she was desirous to have us acquainted, that I was almost forc'd to go; but Resolv'd not to shew my Face. He carry'd *Antonio* to the Park, at an appointed hour, when he said, he heard the Lady say she wou'd be there; and we met 'em as if by chance. We had a Conversation that wou'd have been diverting enough, if my Hatred for him had not made me think, all he did or said disagreeable: He told me I had been continually in his thoughts since he saw me, and that I had made such an Impression in his Heart, as cou'd never be alter'd. I said he must have a strange Opinion of my Credulity if he thought I cou'd believe he was in Love with a Woman he never saw. *Ah!* Madam, *says he* how much more Charming are you Veil'd as you are than a Beautiful Fool that can only please ones Eyes: Such a one as my Friend here made me Visit the other day; and then he gave me a long Description of *Olinda,* and Related all her Discourse; which indeed was very insipid. *We made some Satyrical Remarks upon the poor Lady, and then we* parted, tho' *Antonio* wou'd fain have gone home with us; but we wou'd not permit him. He was very importunate with his Friend after this, to make him acquainted with the unknown; but he said, he durst not carry him to see her without her leave; but he wou'd try to gain it, if he continu'd to desire it, after seeing *Olinda* two or three times. He Reply'd, he wou'd endure so much Mortification, in hopes of so great a Blessing as he promis'd him, but it must be speedy, for a Lover was impatient; and he shou'd be better satisfied with seeing the Ugliest Face he could imagine; than with that doubt he was in. In short, he brought him to our Lodgings several times, and still I acted the Foolish part; but yet he confess'd to his Friend, that I had mov'd him a little; and he Refus'd to see me again for fear he said, that he shou'd Love a

Woman that he cou'd not Esteem: But one moments interview with his other Charmer wou'd deprive *Olinda* of that little part she had gain'd of his Heart. A little after some young Ladies that I knew, were going to the Play, and begg'd me to go with them: I was so chagrin, I cou'd not think of any diversions; but that made them the more pressing, urging it wou'd cure my Melancholy. So I went with them, and the first sight I saw was *Antonio* and his Friend. The last seeing a Lady that was not handsome with me; it came into his thoughts to say, that was she that *Antonio* was in Love with. He gaz'd upon her with the greatest eagerness imaginable, for a long time; then turning to another that was with them; which of those two, *says he*, (pointing to her and me) do you like best? You amaze me with that Question, *Returned he*, for I think there is too great a Disparity between them, to leave any doubt that it must be *Olinda*: (for he knew my Name.) You wou'd alter your Opinion, says *Antonio*, if you knew them both as well as I; for *Olinda*'s Beauty is more than doubly Valu'd by the others Wit, and solid Judgment. But *Olinda* has both, *Replyed the Gentleman*; which I believe you can't but know if you have ever talk'd with, or heard of her: For every body gives her that Character. They Wrong her extreamly, says *Antonio*, for she is really Foolish to deserve Pity; I never Conversed with a Woman whose Company was so tiresome; she talks Eternally, and not one Word of Common Sense. 'Tis impossible your Friend here, who is a very good Judge, has often said such things of her to me, that I must think you mistake the Woman. I have been too often with her for that, says *Antonio*, you may rather believe my Friend Jear'd her. Then they question'd him about it; but he Laugh'd, and said, He never saw a pretty Woman, but he thought she had Wit enough; so that they did not know what to make of him; but *Antonio*, who would not have been sorry to find as much Wit in *Olinda*, as he imagin'd in one, whose outside did not please him so well; took some pleasure in fancying himself deceiv'd; tho' when he consider'd it seriously, he could not believe it. However he enquired diligently of all that cou'd inform him any thing of me, which did more confound him: For they agreed, that I was far from being a Fool, and he cou'd not imagine to what end I shou'd pretend it: But was Resolv'd to find it out. He came often to see us, and still found me the same Fool, till one day when we had a great deal of Company, I was extreamly put to it; for I did not care for making my self ridiculous to so many; and 'twas not good Manners to be silent; however, I chose rather to be Rude, than undeceive him: I often made as if I did not hear when I was spoke to; but I was obliged to Answer, when one said to me, what's the matter with you *Olinda*, that you are Dumb of a sudden? I am sure you ought not; for if it were pardonable in any Woman to talk always, 'twould be in you, that do it so well. I was so confused at this Compliment, that came so *male a propos*; that I believe I did not Answer it over wisely; but as my ill Fate would have it, a Lady in the Company took a Paper out of her Pocket, saying, *I am resolved to make* Olinda *speak whether she will or not; and I will leave you to judge*, whether she does not do it well in this Song. *So she read one that I* had Writ at her desire; for she sung very well. I would fain have denyed it, but I saw it was in vain, for Wit will out one way or other. *Antonio* seemed overjoyed at this Discovery, and I was as much grieved: For no Woman had ever a greater desire to be thought Wise, than I to be thought otherwise. He came to see me every day from that time, and when his Friend told him, that he hoped he would not dispute *Olinda*'s Power any longer, since she made him so absolutely forget her, whom he had once preferred so much to her; he said, that it was not the same *Olinda* whom he loved, for she had chang'd her Soul. Nor had he forgot the other, for it was that Wit, that same turn of Thought, and agreeable Conversation which he admir'd in her, that he ador'd in *Olinda*. I do not know, whether he ever knew, that they were both one Person, but he did not desire to see the other. When he discovered his Love to me, I entertained it so coldly, that he could have little hopes, but that is the last thing that quite forsakes a Lover: And it did not hinder him from persisting. He watched his opportunity, when he saw any thing had pleased me, but still he was Repulsed with greater Scorn. I took delight when he was with me, to Repeat often those Words in *Sophonisba; The* Fort's impregnable, break up your Siege, there is one for you too mighty entered in; the Haughtiest, Bravest, foremost Man on Earth. *He* importuned me extreamly to know who this Happy Man was; and Vowed if I would tell him, he'd never mention his Passion to me again; but I told him, if there was such a Man, it was the same Reason he should trouble me no more, as if he knew who he was; since that could make no alteration in my heart: And perhaps it was a Secret; however, that I would hear no more of his Love. He Begg'd, and Sigh'd, and Whin'd, an Hour or two to make me Reverse my Doom; but in vain; and I was pleas'd that he believed me in Love, tho' I did not think it my self. He continued to Visit me without saying any thing of particular to me; and without suspecting the Object of my Love; 'till my Mother and some Company were talking of the great Actions *Cloridon* had done; just as they Named him, he looked at me, (by chance it may be) but I being a little Guilty, thought it was designed, Blushed, looked down, and was confused, which made me blush the more; and that was enough to fix a Jealousie that had long possest him, and that Watched for the least shadow of Reason to place it upon any particular person. I was so ashamed of my self, that I was not able to stay in the Room, and when I was gone, *Antonio* kept up the Discourse of *Cloridon*; begun to praise his Person, and ask'd my Mother what she thought of him. She said, 'twas so long since she had seen him, that she had almost forgot him; but that her Daughter had seen him lately, (and so told upon what occasion) and that she Extolled him for the finest Man she ever saw. This confirmed his Jealousie; and the first Opportunity he had with me, he told me some News of *Cloridon*: And then asked me if I had ever seen him, and how I liked him. I knew nothing of what my Mother had said; and not being willing he should believe what I found he suspected; I answered, that I had seen him two or three times in Walks at a distance: That I thought he was well enough, but not so handsome as Fame had made him. There needed no more to remove all doubt that he was his Rival; but how to know the particular Terms we were in, was the difficulty; he knew his Character, and thought me Virtuous, and therefore could not fear any thing Criminal betwixt us; but he resolved to try if my Affections were strongly engaged; and to that end he shew'd me a Letter from *Flanders*, wherein it was told him, that *Cloridon* (to the great wonder of all there) had a young Lady disguised in Men's Cloaths with him all the Campagne, and that it was discovered by an Accident, which he gave a large Account of. I found my self seized with an unusual I know not what, and did all my endeavours to conceal it, but I changed Colour two or three times, and he having his Eyes continually upon me 'twas impossible but he must observe my concern: However, he said nothing of it to me, and I forced my self to talk of things indifferent. As soon as I was alone, I examined my self upon the matter. Why should this trouble me (said I within my self) who would not entertain his Love, when it was offered me, and I have often Resolved never to see him, even when I thought him Constant? How comes it then, that I am so Grieved and Angry that he loves another? And that I wish with such impatience for his Return? In fine, I discovered, that what I had called Esteem and Gratitude was Love; and I was as much ashamed of the Discovery, as if it had been known to all the World. I fancyed every one that saw me, read it in my Eyes; And I hated my self, when Jealousie would give me leave to Reason, for my extravagant thoughts and wishes: Mean while *Antonio* would not be Idle, he thought this was the time for him; when my Anger was Raised against *Cloridon*; that and my Obedience to my Mother (if he could get her of his side, which he did not much doubt) would induce me to Marry him; and then he did not fear, but Reason and Duty would overcome my Love. Accordingly he had my Mother's Consent, and entreated her to intercede for him; but all this was so far from having that effect which he expected, that I hated him the more: I was so unjust as to look upon him as the Cause of my Affliction, and I was so Angry to see him take such Measures, as I foresaw must make me very uneasie, that I treated him ill, even to Rudeness. But I will leave him and *Olinda* equally unhappy, till the next Post; and then give you an Account of some Alteration in their Affairs, which if it gave her ease, I believe a little encreased his pains. In the mean time believe, that I remain

Your Friend, Olinda.

'Tis not possible for you to imagine, much less for me to express what I endur'd, by my own Jealousie, and *Antonio*'s Persecution: Either of 'em wou'd have been grievous enough, but together they were intolerable; and I cou'd expect no Remedy, for I knew not what I wou'd have. I did not continue one moment in the same Mind; I long'd for *Cloridon*'s Return, and yet I resolv'd not to see him, tho' when I thought that perhaps he would not desire it, I almost dy'd with the Fear; but that was soon over, for a Week after *Antonio* had shew'd me the Letter I mention'd in my last, he came to Town, and sent me a Letter the first Night, fill'd with the tenderest expressions of Love, and Vows, that all his Fortune and Conquests abroad could not give him the least Joy, whilst I remained inexorable; and a hundred Entreaties to see him once, and he shou'd die contented. This was some satisfaction to me; but 'twas but imperfect: Sometimes I believ'd all he said, and presently after call'd him false and Perjur'd: One while I resolv'd not to answer him, and the next Minute chang'd my Mind; but I was long before I cou'd fix upon what to say. At last I writ with a great deal of affected coldness, only I gave him some dark Hints of the Lady I had heard was with him, which in his Answer he said, he did not understand. He writ several times to me by private Direction, which I had given him when I believ'd he was only my Friend; but a little after he sent to our Lodgings, to tell me, that he had a Place at his disposal, which if I had any Friend that wou'd accept of it, was at my Service. My Mother made me return him Thanks, and tell him, that I had a Relation who was very fit for the Employment, who shou'd wait upon him, but he was not now in Town. *Cloridon*, who desir'd no better occasion, sent me word, that if I wou'd let him see me, he wou'd tell me what was to be done in it; for it was not a thing to be neglected, because there were a great many pretended to it, who might get it by some other means, since it did not wholly depend on him. I did not know what pretence to make to hinder my going, for I durst not tell my Mother of our Meeting without her knowledge: And perhaps I was glad of the necessity of seeing him, since it took away the Fault, and serv'd for an excuse both to my self and him; tho' I was sorry to be forc'd to receive new Obligations from him. I never saw a Man in such an extasie of Joy, as he appear'd to be in at this Interview: He was Speechless and Motionless for a long time, and when he spoke, 'twas with so passionate and charming Words and Air, that I was not able to say those severe things I design'd. I check'd him for obliging me to see him, after I had refus'd him so often, that he might know 'twas contrary to my Inclinations; but (as he told me since) he saw something in my Eyes which made him think, I was not very Angry with him: And when I explain'd that part of my Letter which hinted of the Lady, I did it in such a manner, that he believ'd me Jealous. At first he seem'd amaz'd at what I told him, but afterwards he deny'd it so coldly, and took so little pains to perswade me 'twas false, that I was enrag'd; which still discover'd my Weakness the more. He found one pretence or other for delaying the Business, and for seeing me two or three times, and took pleasure in heightning my Jealousie; till he thought, if he trifled with me any longer, he might lose me for ever: And then he begun to protest seriously, There was no such thing, that it must be the invention of some particular Enemy of his; for if I wou'd give my self the trouble to enquire, I should find it was no general Report, and 'twere impossible it shou'd not be known by every Body, if what I had heard was true. We easily believe what we wish; and when I consider'd from whom I had the Story, I much doubted the truth of it: And whilst I saw him, and heard him Swear, he had never had the least inclination for any other Woman since he saw me. I was firmly perswaded of his Fidelity; but my suspicions return'd a little, as soon as I left him. He told me, he cou'd willingly forgive the Invention, since it had occasion'd the discovery of my Sentiments, which were to his Advantage; but reply'd, That he need not much boast of what my Weakness had reveal'd; for tho' I cou'd not now deny that my Heart took too great a part in what concern'd him, yet since he knew it, nothing shou'd prevail with me to see him again; and so I left him: But I cou'd not forbear saying at parting, that he had made me very unhappy, and I wish'd I had never seen him, tho' I condemn'd my self a hundred times for it afterwards. I ask'd of all I knew that had been in *Flanders*, or had any Correspondence there, if they heard of *Cloridon*'s having a Lady Disguis'd with him; but they assur'd me, there was not so much as the least Report of it, which pretty well satisfied me as to that: For every Action of a Man of his Quality, and in his Post, is so narrowly observ'd, that a thing so extraordinary cou'd not have been a Secret; but yet I was very desirous to know upon what ground that Letter was writ to *Antonio*. However I wou'd not examine him about it, because I saw he suspected my Love already, tho' he had never told me; but still continued my most assidious Humble Servant and Tormentor: And I think I was not much in his Debt, for I really treated the poor Man Barbarously. My Mother gave him all the opportunities she could, and one day that she had some business that would keep her out till Night; she left me at home, and gave Orders that no body should be admitted to see me but *Antonio*. I was so vexed at this Command, that I resolved to revenge my self upon him, and when I heard the Noise of one coming up Stairs, I prepared to give him the rudest Reception I could: I sate Reading with my back towards the Door, and did not rise when he came in, till I saw a Man kneeling by my side; and then without looking towards him, I got up and walked to the other end of the Room. *What, Madam*, says he, *is my* Offence so great? Or do you hate me so much, that you will not hear me ask for Pardon? *I found something in the Voice soft, and moving, which* struck me like one I was accustomed to be pleased with; and turning about, I was amazed, Good God, *cryed I*, is it possible? Are you *Cloridon*; or do I Dream? How could you come here?——, *How could I* forbear coming so long? *interuppted he,* or how can I live a moment from you? I must see you *Olinda,* whatever I hazard, and since you refused to let me a securer way, how could I neglect so favourable an opportunity? *Then I desired to know by what means he knew, that I was* alone; and he told me, that since the last time he saw me, and that I had been so good as to own my self sensible of his Love, he had had a hundred Plots and Contrivances to see me; but found none so feasible as that, which he had put in Execution. He sent a Servant whom he confided much in, and Ordered him to try all means possible to know my Motions when I went out, and when I was at home alone; and he had found the way to gain the favour of a Servant that belonged to the Landlord of the House, (no doubt he feted her well,) and she had engaged to be secret, and to send him word when I was alone; but she did not know for whom she did this Service; only he had told her, that it was a Man of Quality that was in Love with me, and desired to see me privately, to know how I was affected towards him, before he declared himself publickly. He came to her that morning, and she told him, my Mother was gone out, and that she heard her say, she should not come Home 'till Night; so that if he would come with the Person that was to see me, she would be at the Door to conduct him to me: When they came, she told them, that a Gentleman that courted me had been there just now, but she denied that I was at home on purpose to oblige him. I was angry that he should take so little care of my Reputation; but he said, that it was not at all in danger, for no body knew of it but that Servant who would not tell it for her own sake; or if she did, she saw that 'twas all without my Knowledge. That if I would not give my Consent to see him abroad, he should do something more extravagant that might expose both me and him: But if I would, he'd promise never to speak of his Love to me. In sine, by Threatnings and Intreaties, and my own Inclination, I was prevailed with, after I had made him swear not to mention his pretended Passion. Forgive my Frailty, dear *Cleander,* it was not possible for me to refuse the Man I loved any thing that could admit of excuse, and I found or made Arguments enough to sooth my Inclination, and persuade me it was no Fault only to see him. I hastned him away for fear he should be seen with me, but he lingred on for two or three hours and just as he was going I heard *Antonio*'s Voice asking for me, so that he could not go out without meeting him. I was extreamly vexed, but this was no time to fret or chide. I desired him to step into a Closet, which I had in the Room; where I kept my Books, and told him I would contrive a way to be rid of the other quickly. When I had Locked him in, I took my Hoods and seemed to be putting them on, in order to go abroad, so that *Antonio* could not in good Manners stay; but he desired, since he was so unhappy as to be deprived of that satisfaction he expected in my Company, that I would lend him some Book to divert his Melancholy. I told him, that he would have found so little in my Company, that he needed not much mourn for the loss of it: But as my ill Fate would have it, he was so pressing to borrow a Book, that I knew not how to refuse it; I turned the Discourse and sat down, and said, I had altered my Resolution, and would stay at home. *Antonio* wondred at this mighty Favour, he was so unused to receive any from me, that he was Transported at it: He thanked me for it a hundred times, and I believe presaged no little good Fortune for him from such a Change, tho' my way of entertaining him, gave him no great encouragement. If I should give you a particular Account of our Conversation, it would be as impertinent to you, as it was troublesome to me; I will only tell you, I never passed an Hour with half so much pain as that, having for addition to the usual uneasiness his Company made me endure, that of the unseasonableness of the time. Whilst I was fretting at this unhappy Accident, and fearing he would not go away till my Mother came home, our Landlord's Maid came to tell me, there was one below would speak with me: I went down and saw it was that Servant of *Cloridon's*, which he had spoke of to me; he told me, that the King had sent twice for his Lord, and desired me to tell him, that he must of necessity go presently, for the business was of importance. This was a new Vexation; and I staid some time to deliberate what I should do, and at last, resolved to say I was sent for by a Lady that was Sick, that so *Antonio* might be obliged to leave me. But how was I surprized, when I returned and found *Cloridon* in the Room! I needed not dissemble an astonishment, for I was as much amazed to see him there, as if I had not known he was in the House. He advanced towards me, with a Ceremonious Bow, saying, *You have Reason, Madam, to wonder, and to be Angry at me?* but when you know, that it is the general Frailty of Mankind that brought me hither, your goodness sure will pardon me: I mean Love, Madam, Love which makes the Wisest Men guilty of the greatest Irregularities. *I blushed at what he said, not apprehending his design,* and told him his being there, and his Discourse were both so mysterious to me, that I did not know what to answer him. He said, he thought himself obliged to tell the Truth, since my Reputation would be in danger by concealing it: But first he must beg me to pardon the Servant of the House, and not to let her Master know of it; for he having taken a fancy to her, had wheedled her into a Consent, to let him come and see her, tho' the Wench was very honest: That our Family being all abroad, she had brought him into that Room, and hearing me returned, she had put him into the Closet, believing I would go out again: But finding I staid long, he had entertained himself with my Books, and in removing some had thrown down others, the noise of which had made *Antonio* open the Door; and since it was his Fortune to be discovered in a Foolish thing, he hop'd the Gentleman and I, would let it go no further. We gave him our Word for it; and when he was gone, we both sat silent for a long time, each expecting what t'other would say: At last he begun. *Cloridon* was hard put to it, to be forced to discover such a secret; he that has acquired the Reputation of Chast, found out to be so little Nice, as to take such pains, for one of so mean Quality, and one that has not many things to recommend her. You have the Luck, *said I*, to find out *Cloridon's* Intreagues, when no body else knows any thing of 'em: And he may thank his Good Stars his secret falls into such hands; if you are as careful of this, as you have been of that in *Flanders*, which no body but you has ever heard of. *I shall certainly conceal it Madam*, replyed he, *for your Fame sake; for the malicious World would be apt to* fancy his thoughts were something higher than a Dirty Wench, when he was put into your Closet: But I am to believe what you please, and if you tell me you never saw him before, but in Walks at a distance, I won't doubt of it. *I am not much concerned what you, or any thinks of me, says I,* my satisfaction does not depend upon Opinion: And I shall be always happy, as long as I am innocent; whether you believe me so or not. However I owe so much to Truth, to assure you, that whatever designs *Cloridon* had, I knew no more of his coming here than you did, and that I am very Angry at him for it. *If you had not told me so* Madam, I should, it may be, have thought you would rather have lent me a Book, than endured my Company so long (which you always used to avoid) but that you feared I should see him, if you opened the Closet; but I am very glad, you will have me interpret your staying with me more to my advantage. *I was vexed he should think it was to oblige him; and since* I found he was Master against my Will, of the greatest part of my Secret, I thought it best to make him a Confident of it, which would prevent his Addresses to me, and engage him to the greater Fidelity. I told him then, all that was betwixt us; and he gave me some good Counsels, not to cherish a Love, or entertain a Correspondence that might in the end prove dangerous, considering his Circumstances; but I was too far gone to take them, and besides, coming from a Rival, I did not make much Reflexion upon them. Advices by an interested Person, tho' never so reasonable, are not minded, or at least are much suspected, especially when they contradict the inclination of the Advised. I did not tell him, I had consented to see *Cloridon*, because I resolved not to tell him any thing, but what I could not conceal. I did not see *Antonio* in a Month after, but he sent often to ask how we did, and said, *he was very ill himself.* He Writ once to me, to tell me he was endeavouring to overcome a Passion, which he found was displeasing to me, and which therefore must make him very unhappy; and to beg me, if he could effect it, to accept him as a Friend, and not continue that hatred for him then, which I had for my Lover. Mean while, the too Charming *Cloridon* and I met together often: At first we entertained one another with all the News, and little Intreagues of the Town; he put so entire a Confidence in me, was so pleased to see me, and so obliging to me, and my Relations upon all Occasions, that I then thought my self happy, to a degree that left no Room for Wish; for he gave me the greatest evidences of his Love, without speaking of it to me, which was all I could desire from a Man, whose Love I preferred to every thing but Virtue; and who I could not hear talk of it without a Crime: But how easily are we drawn in by such steps as these, to things we had made the strongest Resolutions against. In some time he made Complaints to me, and spoke of his Passion in a third Person, so that I might understand him, but I could not be angry with him; and I knew not how insensibly, and by degrees I accustomed my self to hear of his Love; at first defending my self against it, and chiding him for breaking his Word; but his Excuses seemed to me stronger Reason than my Accusations; and at last I suffered it with Pleasure, and without Reluctancy. Thus my unwary Heart entangled it self more and more, pleasing it self with its own Folly, without looking backward or forward; happy for the present on all sides, for now I was no longer troubled with *Antonio*. He after a Months absence came to see me, and told me, he desired nothing of me now but my Friendship, and to convince me, he was not my Lover, he would tell me a secret in favour of *Cloridon*, if I would promise to forgive him; I told him I would, and then he gave me that Account which I have given you, of his first suspecting my Love, and how to try it, he had feigned that Letter which he shewed me; that he had resolved to undeceive me, as soon as he had discovered what Sentiments I had for him; but when he saw how it affected me, Jealousie would not give him leave, and love prompted him to make use of it to his own Advantage. He added, that tho' Love had made him guilty of Treachery so much contrary to his Nature, yet I should always find him the most sincere, and the most faithful of his Friends. Tho' I believed before that Story to be an invention; you cannot imagine how much I was pleased, to be sure of it now. I easily pardon'd him, since I had promised it, and since I thought he deserved it, having told it voluntary. From that time I received him more favourably than I used to do, and took some pleasure in his Conversation, because he was the only Man that knew of my Love, and that I could talk with freely of *Cloridon*. But now my Mother perceived I had some more complaisance than before for *Antonio*; she wondred he talked nothing of Marriage to her, and told me her thoughts, which put me upon new contrivances, how I might shun her Anger, and yet *Antonio* come off with Honour. I found him raise scruples against all the Methods I would invent, and often he asked me, if I design'd never to Marry, and what Reasons I could always give for not doing it; which made me apprehend he was not altred so much as he seemed; and fear I should have some trouble in this Affair, he had told me, that when he was very young, his Father had contracted him to a kinswoman of his, that lived in the House with them, who had a great Fortune, and he heard was handsome, and witty; but he went to his Travels before it could be known, whether she was either so; that he had never had any Love for her: I had a great mind to let my Mother know this, for I knew she was scrupulous in such things, and would not consent to Marry me to a Man, that had any engagement to another; but I was loath to do it, without his leave, since he was so sincere as to tell it me, and because I was afraid to exasperate him. I took a great deal of Pains to flatter him into a complyance; I told him my Mother could not have the worse Opinion of him for it, since it was a thing done when he was so young, and that he could have no other Reason to hinder him, now that he had no design upon me, which if he had, I should find other ways to disappoint them, tho' perhaps they might make me more uneasie. At last, with much difficulty he agreed to it, and when I told it to my Mother, I found her affected as I wish'd; which when *Antonio* knew, he fetched a great Sigh, and only said, *Have I lost all my hope then, Madam?* and so went away extreamly discomposed. A while after he came to take leave of us, and said his Father had sent for him in haste, to go to his own Country; but he told me in private, that he could stay no longer in a place, where he grew every day more and more unhappy; and that now he had resolved to leave it: He could not forbear telling me, that he had only concealed his Love all this while, to get into my Favour, and in hopes of finding something which might give him hopes. But since I had now deprived him of all, he would not encrease his Misery, by seeing every day the Objects of his Love, and of his Hate, his cruel Mistress, and his happy Rival. I am told his Father presses him extreamly to Marry, being his only Son, but he waves it. I should think I had given you a Description of a Miracle of Constancy in spight of Rigours and Absence; but that in this Age, kindness is a more effectual way to cure Love; an unlucky thing, since no body will attempt it, that has that design; but I, (or Fortune for me,) found you see, a less dangerous way to free my self, with more ease than I could hope, and I think it is time to deliver you now, and give you a little respite till next Post, when you may expect the continuance of the History of

OLINDA.

LETTER VI.

If I did not know to the contrary by my own Experience; you wou'd make me believe, that Friendship and Love can't be contain'd in one Breast. Is it possible you can be so much taken up with *Ambrisia*, that you have not time enough to tell me of it; and that in this Solitude, I should hear of *Cleander's* Affairs from two or three, before I knew any thing of 'em from himself: They tell me you are every day with your New Mistress, and that you are well receiv'd there. I should be pleas'd with it, if I did not fear, instead of finding two Friends, to lose that one, whose Friendship I prefer to all other things: But you'll make me almost Jealous of her if you don't write quickly, for this is my fourth since I've heard from you. Tell me *Cleander*, you that search into the Nature of things, that know the Passions of Men; how they are form'd in the Soul, and by what means, and what Degrees they rise; tell me how I may give that Awe, that fear, or that Respect which I hear often talk'd of, that makes Men not dare to tell a Woman that they love her. Is it the Grave, the Sour, the Proud, or modest Looks? Or is there no such thing, but in Songs and Romances? For my part, I could never meet with it; and tho' perhaps there is some Pleasure in being belov'd, I cannot endure to be told of it, unless by the Language of the Eyes, or so; for that we need not understand: But there's nothing so dull, or so troublesome to me, as a declar'd Lover: This Reflection was occasion'd by an Adventure happen'd to me two days ago; a Stripling of Eighteen, whose Father and Mother had been Servants in the Family where I am, said to one in the House (who told me) that he was in Love with me, and after had the Insolence to tell me himself, that he was in Love; *But you little think* with whom, Madam, *added he; and just as he was going to finish his* Declaration, by good Fortune he was call'd away: Can any thing be more provoking? Teach me where to place my Anger, on the Men, or on my self. *Antonio* was bashful to a Fault in other things, and yet he did not fear to say all he thought, and it may be more to me. *Cloridon*, who treated me with the highest Respect imaginable, discover'd his Love to me, as soon as he knew it himself; and many have pretended it, that never felt any, at least for me. The last indeed had encouragement enough, not to repent of what he had done, and Reason not to despair of any thing he could ask; so that after being two Years contented with my Love, he resolv'd to put it to the Trial, and begun to pretend to Favours, with all the Arguments he could invent, or find, to perswade me of the innocence and lawfulness of what he ask'd: You may find what influence they had upon me by the following Lines, which he sent me in a Letter next day.

    I.

NOT one kind Word, not one relenting Look?
The harsh, the cruel Doom to mitigate?
Your Native Sweetness, ev'n your Eyes forsook;
They shin'd, but in the fiercest form of Hate.

    II.

Is't Honour does these Rigid Laws impose;
That will no sign of gentleness allow;
That tells you 'tis a Crime to pity Foes,
And bids you all the utmost Rigour show?

III.

All Praise the Judge, unwilling to Condemn,
Where Clemency with Justice long Debates:
But he who Rig'rously insults, we blame,
And think the Man more than his Sin, he hates.

IV.

Dare I my Judge accuse of Cruelty?
When at her Feet she saw her Slave implore,
With hasty Joy she gave the sad Decree:
I hate you, and will never see you more.

V.

Ay! 'tis too plain, the false Olinda's *pleas'd*
To see the Captive's Death her Eyes had made:
As what she wish'd, she the Occasion seiz'd;
No Sigh a kind Reluctancy betray'd.

VI.

If you intend to try your Power or Skill,
A Nobler way pursue the great Design:
The meanest Wretch on Earth knows how to kill;
But to preserve from Death's an Act Divine.

VII.

Like Heav'n, you with a Breath can Recreate
Your Creature, that without you does not Live:
Say that you Love, and you r'voke my Fate;
And I'm Immortal if you can forgive.

VIII.

My fiercest Wishes you shall then restrain,
And Love that tramples o'er my Heart subdue:
What doubt can of your mighty Pow'r remain,
When ever that submits and yields to you?

I believe I spoke from my Heart, when I told him I hated him; I'm sure I thought so then, when I saw him whom I believ'd to have an Esteem and Respect for me, act as if he had neither. I said the most violent things I could imagine against him, and left him without the least Reluctancy: But my Rage, or Hate, was soon converted to a Quiet Stupid Grief, that overwhelm'd my Soul, and left me not the Power of easing it the common way, in Tears or Complaints. I saw that I must resolve never to see him again, whatever it made me endure: And in fine, I saw all that could make me unhappy, without any hopes of a Remedy; for tho' he writ to me often to beg my Pardon, and Vow'd a thousand times he wou'd not be guilty of the same fault again, tho' he were sure to be successful; yet I prevail'd with my self absolutely to refuse to see him, with more Resolution than I thought my self capable of; for I consider'd it was dangerous to trust him, notwithstanding his Protestations, since he had broke his Word before: And I don't know if I had not some Reason to distrust my self, after having gone so far, as not only to suffer him to talk to me of his Love, but to own mine to him. When he saw this would not do, he had recourse to his old way of Writing upon Business; but the Letter came first to my Hands, and so I stifled it, and said nothing of it to my Mother. A Week after a Porter came to me, and said he was sent by the Countess of —- who desir'd me to go immediately to her Lodgings, for she had something of great Consequence to tell me, and that he left her at a place where she had Din'd, but she was just going home. Away I went, and when they told me she was not at home, I thought she would not fail of being there presently, and went up Stairs to Stay for her: When I came into the Room, I saw *Cloridon* there, and wou'd have retir'd; but he civilly hinder'd me, and told me, he was waiting for his Cousin (for this Lady was nearly related to him) whom he expected to come in very soon; but 'twas a great happiness I came before, and more than he cou'd have hop'd for from Fortune; for at first he pretended it was Chance brought us together there; but he knew I must find it out, and so to prevent my discovering it to the Lady, he told me, that coming to Visit her, and not finding her at Home; it came into his thoughts to send for me in her Name; for he knew that she us'd to visit me, and often desir'd me to go abroad with her, or to bear her Company at home; so that he hop'd he might succeed without being suspected. I was in great confusion, and very angry at the Trick he had put upon me; and yet I could not but be a little pleas'd at it too. I lov'd to see him, and was glad of an opportunity to give him his Pardon, which I did, but made a Vow never to consent to meet him in private, tho' he begg'd it upon his Knees above an Hour, and said he would not rise till I had granted it: I suppose he was not so good as his Word; but I left him in that posture, and before I went away, and charg'd him not to write to me any more. This Interview serv'd but to increase my melancholy; I indulg'd it a long time, and thought upon nothing but what sooth'd and added to it: But at length considering the occasion of my misfortune, it represented itself to me, not only as my Folly, but my Crime; and then I concluded it must be a Crime to grieve for the loss of that, which 'twas a Crime to Love; and so fix'd a resolution of overcoming my Passion, which I endeavour'd to do by Reason, and by Diversions. Had I had you my Friend to assist me with your Counsels, I had found it much less difficult; but now I had the strongest part of my self to Combat without any Aid: I often gave Ground, and sometimes suffer'd my self to be vanquish'd by the bewitching Reflections of what unequall'd Satisfactions I had found in his Company, and how many happy hours I enjoy'd with him; but some good Thought would rouse my Soul to strive again, and then the Victory was mine. I find by Experience 'tis but bravely, heartily, and thoroughly Resolving upon a thing, and 'tis half done: There's no Passion, no Temptation so strong, but Resolution can overcome: All is to be able to Resolve; there's the Point, for one must lose a little of the first Ardour before one can do that; and many of our Sex have ruin'd themselves, for want of time to think. 'Tis not a constant settled purpose of Virtue will do; there must be particular Resolutions for a particular Attack; 'Tis easie enough to say, no Man shall prevail with me to do an ill thing; the difficulty is, such a Man shall not; he that I love, he that 'tis Death for me to deny any thing to: There I got the better of my self, and as last attain'd to a calm serenity of Mind, which I have enjoy'd ever since, as much as can be expected in such a World as this; and which nothing can disturb, if you continue to have that Friendship for me which you have profess'd, and which your Silence makes me almost doubt of; but there's hardly any thing I could not more easily believe, than that *Cleander* is False or Inconstant. Write quickly, for I am impatient to know the Cause of this unkindness to

Your constant Friend,

OLINDA.

LETTER VII.

AMbrisia's Cruel, Coy, Disdainful, and you believe she hates you; and yet *Ambrisia* took occasion at Play to impose upon you as a Penance, not to write for a Month to one she believ'd you lov'd. If this had been another's Case, you wou'd have discover'd that *Ambrisia's* Jealous. Trust me, she loves you, and only puts on the usual Disguises of Women as sincere as she is; and give me leave to justifie her, and the rest of our Sex in that Case: You have learn'd so well to feign Love, when you have none, that 'tis very hard to discern Art from Nature; and 'tis but reasonable we should be allow'd the less Guilty part of concealing ours, till we can know whether you are sincere: Besides, we know those things are most valu'd, that are obtain'd with most difficulty; and your natural Inconstancy gives us Reason to use all means to make you prize us as much as we can. Your selves too, encourage us in it, for you despise a Woman that's easily gain'd, tho' you rail at the Dissembler; and we can't begin to love just when you would have us; so that both for our own sake and yours, 'tis sometimes necessary to deceive you: And I believe I may add, that there is a Natural Modesty in some Women, that makes 'em asham'd to own their Love. Mr. *Dryden* in his *State of* Innocence, *gives our Mother* Eve *a little of that; tho' some are of* Opinion, it had its Birth from your faithlessness; and that if you had not been false, we had never been shie. If it be so, don't you think we have Reason to be cautious in a thing of such Weight; But I need not take such pains to defend this Cause, for mine was a Fault on the other hand, a too easie discovery of my Love: And to speak the Truth, whatever we are accus'd of, I believe that's the more general one. 'Tis only those that are as Wise as your Mistress, that can have so much Command over themselves, as to be guilty of the 'tother; tho' if she knew you as well as I do, she wou'd find that she has no need to make use of any Arts to try you, or to preserve you: However don't despair, the Mask will soon fall off. You have Reason to wonder at my breaking off with *Orontes*, since by what I have told you, *Cloridon* cou'd be no occasion of it: But suspend your amazement a little, tho' my Misfortunes ended at Seventeen, my Adventures did not, and several things have happenn'd to me in the Year I have pass'd since, which you are yet a Stranger to. You neither know how my Acquaintance begun with *Orontes*, nor why it ended. In the beginning of last Summer, when I was endeavouring to divert my Love and Grief, I went with a Lady to see a Play: She was not in humour to Dress, and would needs have me go *Incognito*; and as we were coming out of the Play-House, we were seiz'd upon by two Sparks, who swore they would not part with us; but that either we should Sup with them, or they wou'd go with us. We did not know how to be rid of these Impertinents, but we saw, if we took Coach, we could not hinder them from going into it; so we resolv'd to walk to our Mantua-maker, who liv'd hard by; and when we went in they left us, as we thought: but a quarter of an hour after, they came up Stairs, and tho' we were very angry at the Rudeness, yet they staid a pretty while; and he that had at first apply'd himself to the other Lady, was very pressing to be acquainted with her; but my Spark sat down just opposite to me without saying a Word, only sometimes desir'd his Friend to go away; which after he had plagu'd us half an Hour, they did: The next Week I went to *Tunbridge* with my Mother; and the first sight I saw at the Wells, was this Gentleman: He came towards us very respectfully, and said he was very glad of this opportunity of begging my Pardon, for the Insolence he had been guilty of; he hop'd the Lady who was with us, whom he had the Honour to know, would intercede for him. She that was in the Country with us, and who you know is an intimate Friend of ours, happen'd to be very well acquainted with him; and when we came home, she told me that his Name was *Orontes*; that he was a Gentleman who had but a small Fortune; but to repair it, he was Marry'd to a rich Widow above Threescore and ten; that tho' she was very ill Natur'd, he was the best Husband in the World to her, but he would take his pleasure abroad sometimes, and she was extreamly Jealous. He came to visit this Lady, and entreated her to carry him to see me; for he said he was sensible of the Affront he had given me the first time he saw me, and that he was very desirous of some Occasion to serve me; and he thought himself obliged to tell me so, and to seek all Opportunities of doing it. She consented to it; and he came often to see us, and was very obliging to us. I will let you know my thoughts of him, because you can tell me if they are just; for he said he was not the same Man with me as with any Body else: He seem'd to me to have Wit enough, but 'twas rough and unpolish'd; nothing of that Politeness which renders a Man agreeable in Conversation. After the common Theams of the Weather, and News were discuss'd, playing at Cards, or taking the Air, were certainly propos'd: But I have heard, that in other places he was very entertaining, and had a hundred pleasant Stories to divert the Company. What can be the reason of this? I am sure he stood in no awe of me, as his future Actions shew'd; and he always told me his Thoughts freely, but plain and blunt, without giving 'em the turn of Gallantry, which is necessary to take; and yet he could not want Breeding, for he always convers'd with People of the First Quality. The Manner is often more look'd upon than the Thing; and tho' I'm as little pleased with Forms as any Woman, yet in some things 'tis the essential part; there are few Men, whose Esteem or Respect I covet; but I would have all Men keep that distance with me, as if I gave 'em Awe; but I could never obtain it of 'em; tho' none ever gave me so much occasion to lament it as *Orontes*. Once, when he was at our Lodging, my Mother was talking of a Journey she design'd the next day about Ten Miles off, where she was to stay all Night: He asked me if I went with her: I said *No*; and desired my Mother to return as soon as she could; because I should be alone till then. It seems (as he told me since) he had made an Appointment with a particular Friend of his about Business of Importance; but having been long desired to see me alone, he would not neglect this Occasion, and sent him an Epistolary Excuse in these Words:

> *My Wife thinks I am with you, but* Olinda *told me she shall be alone* to day, and
> I don't know when I shall meet with so favourable an Opportunity; so that
> you must excuse me; but I'll certainly see you to morrow.

His Wife, being always suspicious of Letters she did not read, went to the Post-House after this: They made no scruple to give it her; because they knew 'twas one of their Servants had brought it; and when she had read it, she went home in all haste, and had her Husband dog'd to my Lodgings. When he came there he told me, that the first time he saw me, he lik'd my Shape and Mien, and was extreamly taken with my Face, that he durst not so much as ask me Pardon whilst he saw me so angry; and that since he was acquainted with me, my Humour had charm'd him so, that he could be content to leave all the World for me: And then, Laughing, ask'd me, If I could live with him, and he would keep me a Coach, and let me want nothing I could desire. I rally'd with him till he begun to talk more seriously, and then I check'd him for his Insolence; but it had no effect upon him; And when he saw that neither Promises nor Intreaties could move me, and that Opportunity favour'd him, he resolved to try what Violence would do; he had sent our Servant a Mile off for to fetch some Fruit, which, he said, was the best about the Country; and we were in a back Room near no Body in the House, so that I was in great Fear; however I made all the noise and Resistance I could, and was happily delivered by his old Lady's coming in: She might easily perceive we were both in Confusion, tho' she hardly guess'd the true Cause; and I was so good natur'd as not to tell it her. When she rail'd, we bore it with a great deal of Patience, and indeed I wonder'd at his Moderation: I really thought he would have let her beat me to revenge his Cause; but he was not so much a Brute, he hinder'd her, and very civilly led her away. The next day I saw him at the Wells, and whilst my Company was Raffling, he took the opportunity to talk with me, though I avoided him with all the Diligence I could. *Don't frown upon me, Olinda,* says he, *you ought to forgive me; Repentance is all that Heaven requires, and I* never in my Life did an Action that troubled me so much; but if you have not good Nature enough to pardon me upon that, I must say something to excuse my self: If I believ'd you Virtuous before, it must be by an implicit Faith; but the way to be sure was to try it; and now I shall always admire that Virtue I could not subdue: Why then should you be angry with me any longer than my Fault remains? *Though I had a little* Prejudice against him, I thought he spoke with more Eloquence, and a better Grace, than ever I heard him before; it may be his Concern inspir'd him; but 'twas to little purpose, for I was inexorable. I told him, *I did not think him worth my Anger, and should easily forgive him,* upon Condition he would never see me any more: No, *Madam, said he,* I'd rather see you angry, than not see you at all: *But in spight of me, he* visited us often; but I always entertain'd him with a coldness that did not much please him, though no Body else perceiv'd it. We came to Town in the beginning of *September,* and he was once at our House, and found me alone: He began to talk of a violent Passion he had for me; but I stop'd him, and said, *That was not a Discourse fit for me to hear from* him. *I commanded him to leave me; and told him if he ever came there* again, I wou'd be deny'd to him. He obey'd me, and I did not see him again till *November.* He came in Mourning, and told us he had had the misfortune to bury his Wife. He Writ to my Mother to desire her leave to make his Addresses to me; which she gave him, and then he appear'd a declar'd Lover. I was so us'd to receive him with Anger and Disdain, that though I had not the same Reason now, I did not change my Behaviour to him; and for four Months my Mother let me take my own way, without speaking one word of *Orontes* to me: Either she design'd to observe what I wou'd do of my self, or she did not think it fit to talk of my Marrying him so soon after his Wife's Death; but when she saw I slighted him so long, she said to me one day, What do you mean Child, to receive with equal indifference all the Proposals that are made to you? Do you resolve to lead a single Life? I should approve of the choice in one of a better Fortune; but you must conform your self to yours, and consider that I am not able to maintain you. If you don't hate *Orontes,* I will have you Marry him, he has given so great proof of his being a good Husband, that you can't fear he will be otherwise to you; he is Handsome enough, and very Rich; I believe he loves you, and in fine, I think you may be as happy with him as with any Man; therefore, don't be obstinately bent against your own good. He came in at the same time, and seconded this command of my Mothers with Intreaties and Complaints. I had no Aversion for him, and since my Circumstances wou'd oblige me to Marry, and that I knew I could never love any Man; I thought it might as well be he as any other; so in sometime after I yielded, and the Wedding-day was appointed to be the Sixteenth of *May* last. How do you think 'tis possible to avoid it now; but many things happen betwixt the Cup and the Lip. You are to know that *Orontes's* Estate lay near a fine Seat of *Cloridon's,* which he often retir'd to; so that they were acquainted, and much together; and that *Orontes* went to his Country House to make some Preparations a Week before the designed Marriage. *Cloridon* told him he was extreamly pleas'd to see him there; for they had made a match for Hunting five or six days after with some Friends of his, that were wishing for him. I must beg your Pardon my Lord, *says he, that I cannot stay so long; for I have business that will call me* to *London* sooner. If it be not of great importance, *return'd he,* pray let me prevail with you to stay. 'Tis not to be deferr'd my Lord, I am to be Marry'd. Marry'd, cry'd my Lord, prithee what Madness possesses thee, so lately freed, to bind thy self again without any necessity for it? What Bait next, not another old Rich crabbed Widow, I hope? I have made a better Choice now, *answer'd Orontes:* She has Youth and Goodness I'm sure; and I have Money enough for us both. You are in the Right, *Reply'd Cloridon;* but may I know her Name. You knew her Father my Lord, *says he,* and then Sir *Martin Marrall* told him whose Daughter I was. And are you engag'd to her, *Cloridon* ask'd? She has promis'd to marry me the 16th of this Month, *said Orontes,* and therefore my Lord, I hope you wont take it ill if I leave you upon so weighty an Affair. *Cloridon* was not in humour of making many Compliments; but he ask'd abundance of Questions, of the beginning and progress of his Love, and how I had us'd him all the time; but he could not much boast of my Favour, which pleas'd *Cloridon,* and encourag'd him to endeavour to break off the Match. He told *Orontes* he should be oblig'd to go to *London* that day, but he would come back again before he went away; so he left him, and immediately took his Journey; and as soon as he arriv'd, came to our Lodgings, where he found my Mother and I together. Judge of my surprize at this Sight, my first Thoughts were of *Orontes;* I sigh'd when I compar'd 'em with one another, and had a thousand different thoughts which I know not what to make of. *Cloridon* Addressing himself to my Mother, *said,* Madam, I am come to beg a Favour of you, which I should hardly have the Confidence to ask, if the whole satisfaction of my life did not depend upon it. My Mother told him, that she could not refuse any thing to one whom she ow'd so much to; and that she should think her self happy if she could serve him in a thing which he said concern'd him so nearly. He return'd some Compliments, and then desir'd her to hear him out with Patience, which she promis'd, and he begun, I have a long time had a great Love and Respect for your Daughter, and would have given all the World to have seen her sometimes; but she refus'd it me; and I bore her Rigour without Murmuring, in hopes the time would come when I could tell her I lov'd her without offending her Virtue: But I can't live when I have lost that hope, and therefore am come to beg you not to marry *Olinda*, as I am told you design; and I will make her Fortune greater than what she can expect from *Orontes*. How, my Lord, *interrupted my Mother*, what strange Proposition is this you make me? Be not angry with me, or fear me, *continu'd he*, for the moment you grant what I intreat of you, I will leave you, and never desire to see *Olinda* again, as long as I continue in the Condition I am in; But 'twill be a great Happiness for me to think, that she may one Day be mine; and to be assur'd she will never be any others; and if she be not chang'd, or that I am not much mistaken in her, she will not be averse to it. He was in the right, for though I was never an Enemy to Marriage, yet I always preferr'd a single Life to it; and I found enough of my stifled Flame revive to make my Wishes comply with his. When my Mother saw me much inclin'd to it, and knowing I had only consented to marry *Orontes* in compliance of her; she began to think of it as a thing might be done, but that she had given her Word to *Orontes*, and could not go back from it. But *Cloridon* told her, she need not be in any Fault in that, if she wou'd but make use of the occasion would be given her to break off with *Orontes* without Examining further. She made some other Objections, but he Answer'd them all, and upon his Knees Swore, that if I Married *Orontes*, neither he nor my Husband would survive it: So partly out of fear of what might happen, and partly out of inclination to oblige him, and willingness to please me, my Mother consented. *Cloridon* begg'd leave to talk with me, before he took his last leave, which he did, and made me some little tender Reproaches, for having resolv'd to Marry; which I answer'd with a more reserv'd Kindness than I had sometimes done; and that was the Subject of many Letters he sent me since; for he often writes to me. Two Days before we were to be Marry'd, *Orontes* was to come to Town, which *Cloridon* knew, and had provided half a dozen Soldiers to seize upon him in the King's Name, (for he was suspected for an Enemy to the Government.) They did so, and told him they were commanded to keep him a close Prisoner in a House hard by, till further Order. He would fain have Writ, but they would not let him, for they said they had Orders to the contrary. There they kept him a Week, and we wonder'd we heard nothing of him, not knowing what methods were us'd to hinder us; and to avoid seeing our Friends, who would enquire the Reason, we thought it best to retire hither, this being a private Place. When *Cloridon* knew I was out of Town, he went himself to free him, and told him things had been misrepresented, and he had been wrong'd; but in requital he would procure him any Employment he would name; but he did not accept it. When he came to enquire for me, no Body could tell him where I was: But a Friend with whom I had left such Orders, told him, that I had taken it so ill, that he should slight me so far, as neither to come, nor to send to me, in so long time, that whatever he could say for himself, I wou'd never forgive him, nor so much as hear him. He was no doubt troubled at it, but he was not a Man to take any thing much to Heart; and *Cloridon* knowing he had not dealt very fairly by him, was very desirous to oblige him some other way: And indeed he did him a very considerable Service not long after, for he was really accus'd privately to the King of a Plot, which wou'd have cost him his Life, if *Cloridon* had not taken a great deal of pains to free him, more than he could have expected in such a ticklish Affair as that; and had like to become himself suspected by it: So that I think he has been more his Friend in saving his Life, than he was his Enemy in taking his Mistress from him. This is, *Cleander*, the true Cause of my Retirement, which is very agreeable to me, whilst I hear often from you, and whilst *Cloridon* continues to think of me. I have sent you a Copy of Verses which he writ to me just after I came hither.

> *Nor cou'd my Rival, when those Charms*
> *By thee were destin'd to his Arms,*

Be half so bless'd as I, to find
The lovely Nun for me Confin'd:
Nor when of all that Bliss bereav'd,
He saw his full-blown hopes deceiv'd,
Cou'd be so curst as I to see
My self Exil'd from Heav'n in thee.
Strange Contradiction in my Fate,
At once a blest and wretched State:
But who--what Lover wou'd not choose
Thus to gain all, tho' all he lose?
So Merchants strive their Lives to save,
Threaten'd by ev'ry Wind and Wave,
And see with joy the long'd for Coast,
Tho' all they ventur'd for is lost.

Cloridon has just sent me word that *Orontes* is dead of the Small-Pox; so that I shall come to Town sooner than I design'd. The expectation of seeing you pleases me extreamly; for tho' I find a great satisfaction in conversing with you by Letters; yet 'tis not so full and perfect at this distance, as when I am with you. I can't tell you my Thoughts so well, nor know yours; a Question suddenly started, or sometimes a Look, will discover more to me than you know of your self; and I would know you not as you seem to the World, or what you think of your self, but what you are; for though you are more sincere than other Men, yet there is no Man but deceives the World in some things, and himself in more; and therefore to be a good Man, 'tis absolutely necessary to have a true Friend; and since you have made choice of me, I can only attone for my want of other Qualifications, by my Fidelity, which you may always rely upon. Will not the World, when they see so tender, so constant an Affection betwixt us, be convinced of that receiv'd Error, that there can be no such intimacy betwixt two of different Sexes without the Passion of Love; In us I'm sure they can't suspect it; when they see you have so much Love for *Ambrisia*, and me so forward to promote its being reciprocal. I wish it may have that Effect, that the Women may no longer scruple to bestow their Friendship upon a Worthy Man, for fear of misconstructions; both Sexes will find their Advantages by it. Yours is more capable to instruct and form our Minds; than the wisest of our own; and ours will be more apt to curb that Licentiousness, which Men usually encourage one another in: And what happiness will it be for us to see our selves the Instruments of all the Men's becoming Good, and all the Women Wise? (A more extraordinary Reformation than *Luther*'s.) Let our Friendships then be so Exemplary, that all may emulate, and wish to live like us; and by endeavouring, find that there's a purer and more solid Satisfaction one moment with a Friend, than Ages thrown away upon the Gallantries, which so take up the Hearts, and steal the Hours of our Youth. Adieu *Cleander*, correct the Errors of my Life with a gentle Hand of Friendship, and always be as much my Friend as I am yours,

    OLINDA.

LETTER VIII.

Olinda *to* Cloridon.

In Answer to a Letter which he sent her with the Copy of Verses in the sixth of the foregoing ones.

'TIS not an Hour ago since I believ'd I hated you: I thought I could have rail'd at you, have call'd you base, seducer of my Honour, Traytor, that under a pretence of Love, design'd my Ruin; but Ah! those tender Excuses which you sent me, soon discover'd the mistake, and show'd me it was only Angry Love, that so Transported me: And now 'tis turn'd to as violent a Grief, which wou'd fain ease it self in Complaints: But I am so wretched, that even that poor Comfort is deny'd me; for who can I complain to, when in lamenting my Misfortune I must expose our Crime: For yours my Lord, has involv'd me in the guilt; and all those thoughts and Actions, which were innocent before, must be condemn'd as the Causes of such ill Effects: For if I had never lov'd you, or if I had never own'd it, nor consented to see you, you had not desir'd any thing of me that could shock my Virtue: Now, I can't think of 'em without Shame and Anger. That Love which shin'd before so Pure and Bright, appears now the Blackest thing in Nature; and I hate my self for not hating you; for I own (tho' I blush in owning) that I love you still; Nay, I believe that I forgive you too; but I must never, never see you more: No, though you swear you Repent, and that you would not repeat your Crime, if you were certain of success. Would not you believe I should as easily Pardon your breach of this Vow, as I did the last, which you made me as solemnly? Yes, you would, my Lord, and I should be betray'd to things I never thought of yet: For all is solid, convincing Reason that you speak; and I should soon believe any thing you would have me. Curse on that fond Credulity that first deceiv'd me into a belief, that 'twas no Sin to love you. Yet sure it could not be an unpardonable Fault, to value one that so infinitely deserves it: To Love, to See, and Talk with one whose Conversation is so Charming as yours; and that was all I wish'd. All that know you do the same; Why then am I more guilty? Ah! If your Fame had been as pure as mine, we had both been Happy and Innocent; so innocent, that she, that happy she, who claims all your love as her due, (even she, I think, if she had known our Hearts) could not have been offended at it: But who is there, the most uninterested, that would not now condemn us; Nay, the most Partial could not excuse us; even we should blame our selves. Why will you then importune me still to see you; ask me no more, what I dare never grant; and believe-—but you know, 'tis not unkindness makes me Refuse you: You know I must be Wretched in your Absence; yet think me easie and satisfied, if it will contribute any thing to your quiet; or rather don't think of me at all. Let us make our selves as happy as we can; I will endeavour to forget you; don't Write to me, if you love me well enough to forbear it: And if you can cease to love me, without hating me; for I don't find I have force enough to bear so great a misfortune, which is the only one can add to the weight of those which have already almost sunk

The Poor

OLINDA.